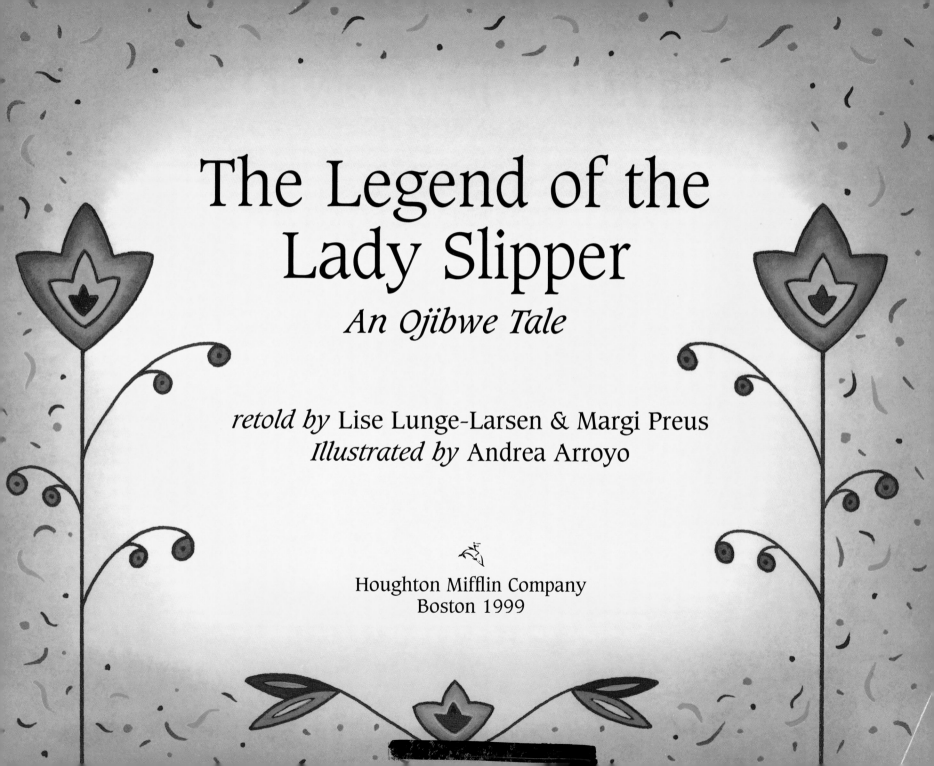

The Legend of the Lady Slipper

An Ojibwe Tale

retold by Lise Lunge-Larsen & Margi Preus
Illustrated by Andrea Arroyo

Houghton Mifflin Company
Boston 1999

Text copyright © 1999 by Lise Lunge-Larsen and Margi Preus
Illustrations copyright © 1999 by Andrea Arroyo

The text of this book is set in Caxton Light.
The illustrations are watercolors, reproduced in full color.

Library of Congress Cataloging-in-Publication Data

Lunge-Larsen, Lise.
      The legend of the lady slipper: an Ojibwe tale / retold by Lise Lunge-
   Larsen and Margi Preus; illustrated by Andrea Arroyo.
         p. cm.
      Summary: In this retelling of an Ojibwe tale, a girl's act of bravery to save
her family leads to the appearance in the world of the delicate and tender flower
called the lady slipper.
         ISBN 0-395-90512-5
      1. Ojibwa Indians—Folklore. 2. Tales—North America. [1. Ojibwa
Indians—Folklore. 2. Indians of North America—Folklore. 3. Folklore—United
States.]
I. Preus, Margi. II. Arroyo, Andrea, ill. III. Title.
E99.C6L85 1999   398.2'089'973—dc21
97-47209   CIP AC

Printed in Singapore
TWP 10 9 8 7 6 5 4 3 2 1

Sources

The Legend of the Lady Slipper is drawn from three different sources: *Chippewa Dawn: Legends of an Indian People,* by Don Spavin; *Giving: Ojibwe Stories and Legends from the Children of Curve Lake,* edited by Georgia Elston; and *Ojibwe Heritage,* by Basil Johnston. In the retelling of this story, David "Niib" Aubid, Ojibwe language instructor, University of Minnesota at Duluth, was especially helpful in showing us how to make the words—particularly the verbs—reflect an Ojibwe understanding of the world as an animate, living place. Special thanks go to him and also to Shelly Ceglar, Ojibwe language instructor, College of St. Scholastica, Duluth, for her time and help.

Densmore, Frances. *Chippewa Customs.* St. Paul: Minnesota Historical Society, 1929.

———. *How Indians Use Wild Plants for Food, Medicine, Crafts.* New York: Dover, 1928, 1974.

Elston, Georgia, ed. *Giving: Ojibwe Stories and Legends from the Children of Curve Lake.* Lakefield, Ont.: Waapoone, 1985.

Hilger, M. Inez. *Chippewa Childlife.* St. Paul: Minnesota Historical Society, 1992.

Imes, Rick. *Wildflower Identifier.* New York: Quintet Publishing, 1989.

Johnston, Basil. *Ojibwa Heritage.* Lincoln: University of Nebraska Press, 1976.

Meeker, James E., Joan E. Elias, and John A. Heim. *Plants Used by the Great Lakes Ojibwa.* Odanah, Wis.: Great Lakes Indian Fish and Wildlife Commission, 1993.

Moyle, John B., and Evelyn W. Moyle. *Northland Wildflowers.* Minneapolis: University of Minnesota Press, 1977.

Nichols, John D., and Earl Nyholm. *A Concise Dictionary of Minnesota Ojibwe.* Minneapolis: University of Minnesota Press, 1995.

Roberts, June Carver. *Born in the Spring: A Collection of Spring Wildflowers.* Athens: Ohio University Press, 1976.

Smith, Welby R. *Orchids of Minnesota.* Minneapolis: University of Minnesota Press, 1993.

Spavin, Don. *Chippewa Dawn: Legends of an Indian People.* Stillwater, Minn.: Voyageur, 1977.

Stensaas, Mark. *Canoe Country Flora.* Duluth, Minn.: Pfeifer-Hamilton, 1996.

Foreword

After the snow has melted in the northern forests, you may chance upon graceful flowers shaped like tiny moccasins. Some are yellow and some are white, some are pink and some are both pink and white. All are lady slippers, the most rare and precious flowers of the north.

This delicate plant grows from the soggy ground of a black spruce bog or the rocky soil of a jack pine forest. It takes fourteen years before the first bloom appears. If left undisturbed it will grow into a thick cluster of flowers which will bloom for another hundred years or more. However, if any part of the lady slipper is picked, the entire plant dies.

How did such a delicate flower come to grow in such rugged country? This Ojibwe legend will tell you.

Once there was a young girl who lived with her mother and father, sister and brother, aunts and uncles, her many cousins, her grandfathers and grandmothers, and all of her people in a village among the whispering pines. Of all her family, her older brother was her favorite.

He was as strong as a bear, as fast as a rabbit, and as smart as a fox. Because of these traits, he was the messenger for the village. When he went on his journeys the little girl begged to go along with him, but all he would say was, "Maybe tomorrow."

Then one day a terrible disease struck. The little girl watched as, one by one, her people became ill. Her grandparents, her aunts and uncles, her sister, her mother. Even her father fell ill.

A neighboring village had the *mash-ki-ki,* the healing herbs,
they needed, but the journey was too dangerous to make in winter.
It was too cold, the snow was too heavy, and between the villages
lay a deep, dark lake covered with groaning ice. Such journeys
were not made in *Gichi-Manidoo Giizis,* the Great Spirit Moon.

Still, her brother said, yes, he would make the trip.

But then even he became ill.

Now the little girl thought surely there was no one else to go, unless she herself were to make the journey. Maybe tomorrow, she thought. But looking at her brother, his face bright with fever, she knew she had to leave right away.

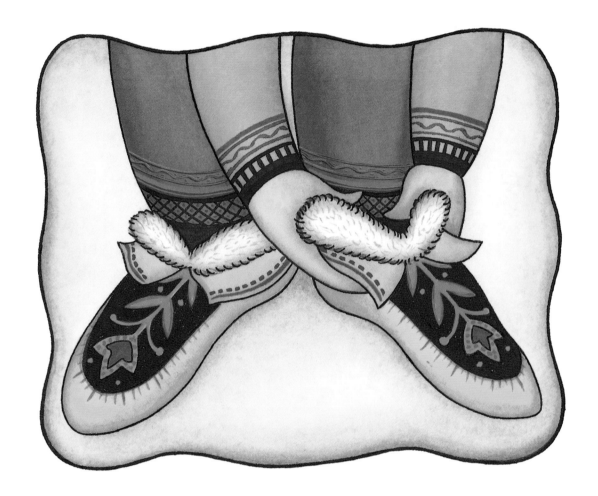

She found her *ma-ki-sins,* the beautifully beaded moccasins her mother had made out of deerskin, and tucked warm rabbit fur inside them. Then she slipped them on and stepped out into a raging storm.

Trees lashed about in the wind, rattling their branches. Falling snow stung her face. "*Mash-ka-wi-zin,*" it hissed, "Be strong."

The girl bent her head and stalked like a bear into the storm. The snow tugged at her, but she charged through it, plunging into the wind.

All day she walked until, at dusk, she stood before the windswept lake. The slick ice lay as if asleep, silent. On the far shore the wigwams of the other village glowed warmly.

The little girl stepped out onto the frozen lake and the ice shuddered and woke. "*Da-daa-ta-biin,*" it rumbled, "Go quickly!"

So the girl ran like a rabbit, skittering and slipping.

When she reached the other side, all the people rushed out to meet her. She told them her story, and when she finished, she saw their faces glowing with admiration.

Then an old woman swept her up and carried her into a lodge. She fed the little girl roasted venison and warm tea. She tucked her in with soft robes. The girl was almost asleep when she remembered the medicines.

"The *mash-ki-ki*," she murmured.

"We will bring you and the *mash-ki-ki* to your people," the old woman whispered. "Tomorrow. It is too dark and too cold to travel tonight."

But when the little girl closed her eyes she saw the sad, pale faces of her family, her friends, and her brother, and she knew she must leave right away. She rose quietly, gathered up the medicine bundle, and crept out.

The storm had stopped. Now all was deep cold and silence, except the popping and cracking of the trees. Her eyes stung; she felt the frost gather on her cheeks. She pulled her robe tight and hurried across the lake.

Blue and green lights flickered in the sky. She knew the lights were the spirits of the dead, gaily dressed, rising and falling in the steps of a dance. *Jii-ba-yag-nii-mi-wag,* her people called them, the northern lights.

What if someone from her family or one of her people were to join them because she had been so slow? She left the lake and quickened her pace, keeping her eyes on the lights in the sky.

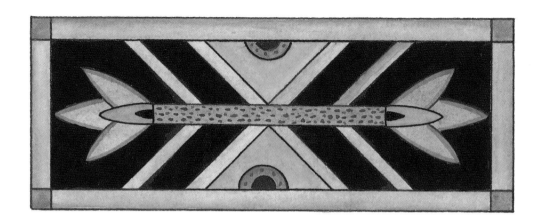

Suddenly, the snow collapsed around her and she was buried up to her arms. She kicked and punched at the snow. That was no use. She churned her little legs as fast as she could, as if to run out of the snow. That only dug her in deeper.

Above her the dancing spirits leapt and spun. Maybe she would be the next one among them, she thought. She fell back, exhausted.

"*Nib-waa-kaan!*" the snow around her whispered, "Be wise!" Yes, she must be smart like the fox who *thinks* his way around the trap.

She lay back to think and felt the snow relax its grip. She lay further back and it let go a little more. Slowly, she wriggled and turned, paddled and swam her way out of the snow.

"*Ho-whah!*" she sang out. Her feet were free!

But then, "*Gaa-wiin!* Oh, no!" she cried. Her feet were bare and cold. Her moccasins were gone, buried deep in the drift. She dug in the snow, but it was too soft and loose. She wiped her nose on her sleeve and continued on barefoot.

With the very first step, icy crystals
cut into her flesh and her feet began to bleed.
In every footprint bright red drops of blood mingled
with the white snow. Still, she stumbled ahead until dawn,
when she reached the edge of her village. There she called out
before sinking into the snow.

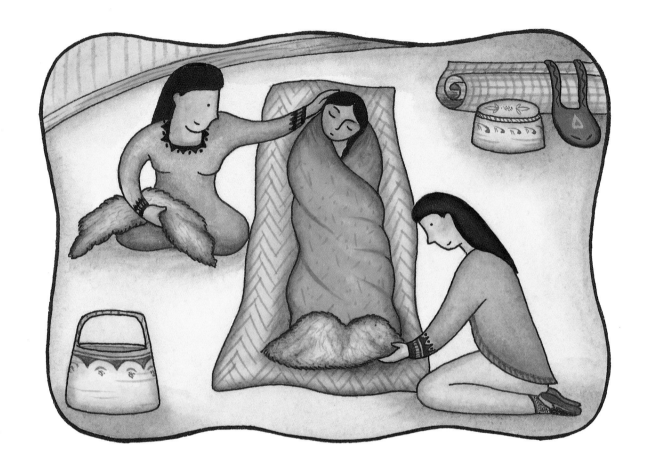

The people from her village—even some of the sick ones—
ran out when they heard her cry. They carried her back to her
lodge and wrapped her swollen and bleeding feet in thick, warm
deerskins.

Because of the *mash-ki-ki,* the people were healed. The little girl remained weak for a long, long time, but soon after the snow melted, she too recovered.

When the forest turned green, she and her brother went to search for her lost moccasins. What they found there filled them with wonder.

On the very spot where she had lost her moccasins and wherever she had stepped with her bleeding feet, beautiful new flowers grew. They were pink and white and shaped just like the little moccasins the girl had worn on her journey.

The Ojibwe people named the new flower *ma-ki-sin waa-big-waan,* which means the moccasin flower. Today it is also called the lady slipper. The people gave the little girl her name, too, "*Wah-Oh-Nay,*" or "Little Flower," because although she was as strong as a bear, fast as a rabbit, and smart as a fox, she was also as lovely and rare as a wild spring flower.